# RULES OF SUMMER

## Shaun Tan

# RULES OF SUMMER

ARTHUR A. LEVINE BOOKS
AN IMPRINT OF SCHOLASTIC INC.

This is what I learned last summer:

Never leave a red sock on the clothesline.

Never eat the last olive at a party.

Never drop your jar.

Never leave the back door open overnight.

Never step on a snail.

Never be late for a parade.

Never ruin a perfect plan.

Never argue with an umpire.

Never forget the password.

Never give your keys to a stranger.

Never ask for a reason.

Never lose a fight.

Never wait for an apology.

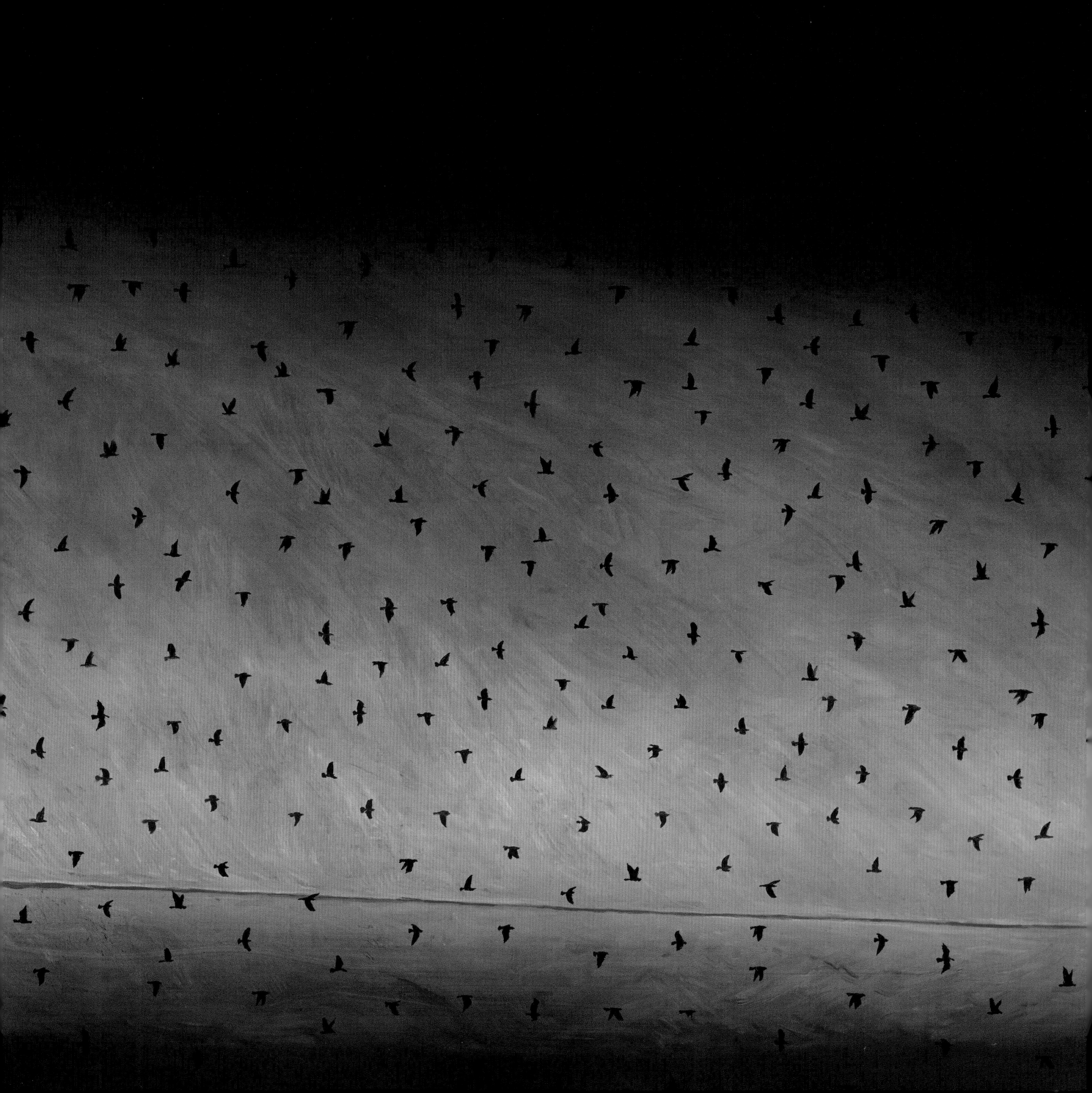

Always bring bolt cutters.

Always know the way home.

Never miss the last day of summer.

That's it.

For the little and the big.

All rights reserved. Published by Arthur A. Levine Books, an imprint of Scholastic Inc., *Publishers since 1920*.
SCHOLASTIC, the LANTERN LOGO, and associated logos are trademarks and/or registered trademarks of Scholastic Inc.

Library of Congress Cataloging-in-Publication Data

Tan, Shaun, author, illustrator.
Rules of summer / Shaun Tan. – First American edition. pages cm
Summary: Two boys explain the occasionally mysterious "rules" they learned over the summer,
like never eat the last olive at a party, never ruin a perfect plan, and never give your keys to a stranger.
ISBN 978-0-545-63912-5 (hardcover : alk. paper) 1. Friendship–Juvenile fiction. 2. Summer–Juvenile fiction.
3. Conduct of life–Juvenile fiction. [1. Friendship–Fiction. 2. Summer–Fiction.
3. Conduct of life–Fiction.] I. Title.

PZ7.T16123Ru 2014
823.92–dc23
2013040915

Book design by Shaun Tan and Phil Falco

10 9 8 7 6 5 4 3 2 1     14 15 16 17 18

First American edition, May 2014

Printed in the U.S.A.    88